D1283416

Hi,
Jeanne!
(TZ rocks!)

Wishing you
a Clean
future!

Fondly,
Betsy
12·17·11

Hole in the Bottom of the Sea

A Song by Christine Lavin

Illustrated by Betsy Franco Feeney

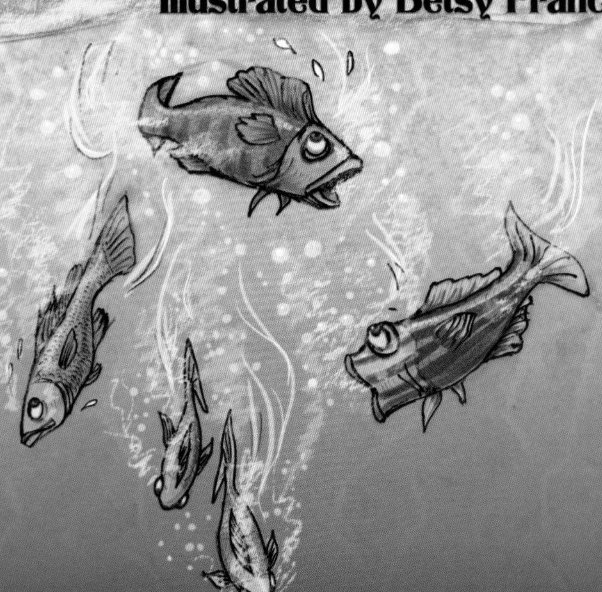

Puddle Jump Press
Nyack, NY

First published in the United States of America by Puddle Jump Press, 763 Rte. 9W, Nyack, NY 10960
www.puddlejumppress.com

All rights reserved. No part of this book may be reproduced or transmitted in any form or by any means, electronic or mechanical, including photocopying, recording, or by any information storage or retrieval system, without written permission from the publisher.

Illustrations are rendered in pencil, acrylic and Adobe Photoshop

Edited by Patricia McHugh and Kathryn Feeney

Special thanks to my husband, Jim, who has supported my every endeavor, and to the members of the Rockland/Bergen/Westchester Scribblers (www.thescribblers.org)
– B. F. F.

Text copyright © 2012 Christine Lavin for the song "Hole in the Bottom of the Sea"
Appendix text and all illustrations copyright © 2012 Betsy Franco Feeney

Publishers's Cataloging-in-Publication Data
Lavin, Christine

Hole in the bottom of the sea / a song by Christine Lavin : illustrated by Betsy Franco Feeney. – 1st ed. p. cm.

Summary: All-new lyrics to a traditional tune make a case for clean energy in response to the devastating impact of the 2010 BP Gulf of Mexico oil spill on marine wildlife. Includes a music CD, lyrics, and an illustrated, educational appendix.

LCCN 2011914388
ISBN 978-097-264878-3
first edition

1. Disasters – Juvenile Fiction. 2. Renewable energy sources – Juvenile Fiction.
3. Marine animals – Juvenile Fiction. 4. Stories in rhyme.
I. Franco-Feeney, Betsy. II. Title.

PZ7.L3526Ho2011

[E] – dc22

Printed in China by Broad Link Enterprise Ltd.

This one's for you, Chris
– B. F. F.

And I dedicate this book to Edith and Ervin Drake,
who grace the recording with their voices
and the world with their presence
– C. L.

There's a hole in the bottom of the sea
A hole in the bottom of the sea
There's a hole

There's a hole

A hole in the bottom of the sea.

There's a pipe in the hole
in the bottom of the sea

A pipe in the hole
in the bottom of the sea

There's a hole,
There's a hole,

A hole in the bottom
of the sea.

There's a crack in the pipe in the hole
in the bottom of the sea

A crack in the pipe in the hole
in the bottom of the sea

There's a crack
In the pipe
In the hole in the bottom of the sea.

There's a dolphin in the oil
on the surface of the sea

A dolphin in the oil
on the surface of the sea

There is oil,
There is oil,

Oil on the surface of the sea.

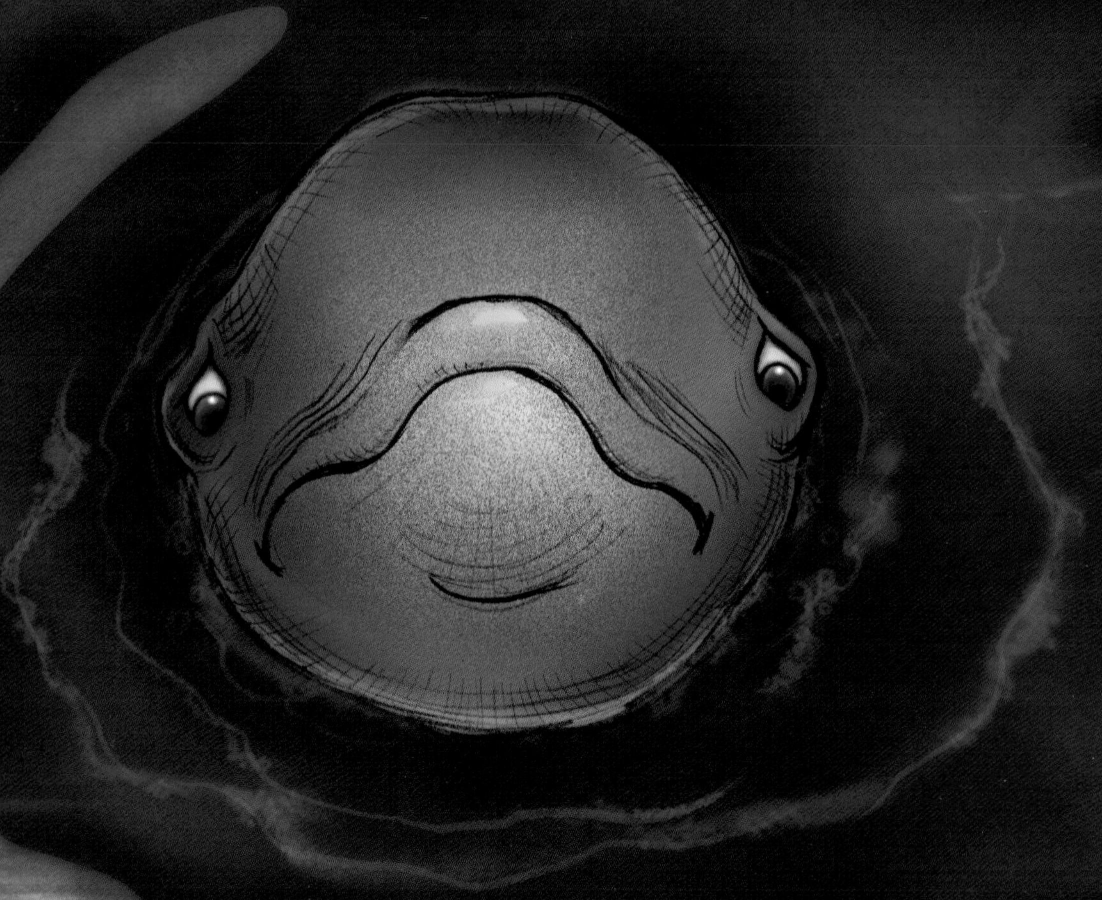

There's a bird on a dolphin in the oil
on the surface of the sea

A bird on a dolphin in the oil
on the surface of the sea

There is oil
There is oil

Oil on the surface of the sea.

There's a turtle on a bird on a dolphin
in the oil on the surface of the sea

A turtle on a bird on a dolphin
in the oil on the surface of the sea

There is oil
There is oil

Oil on the surface of the sea.

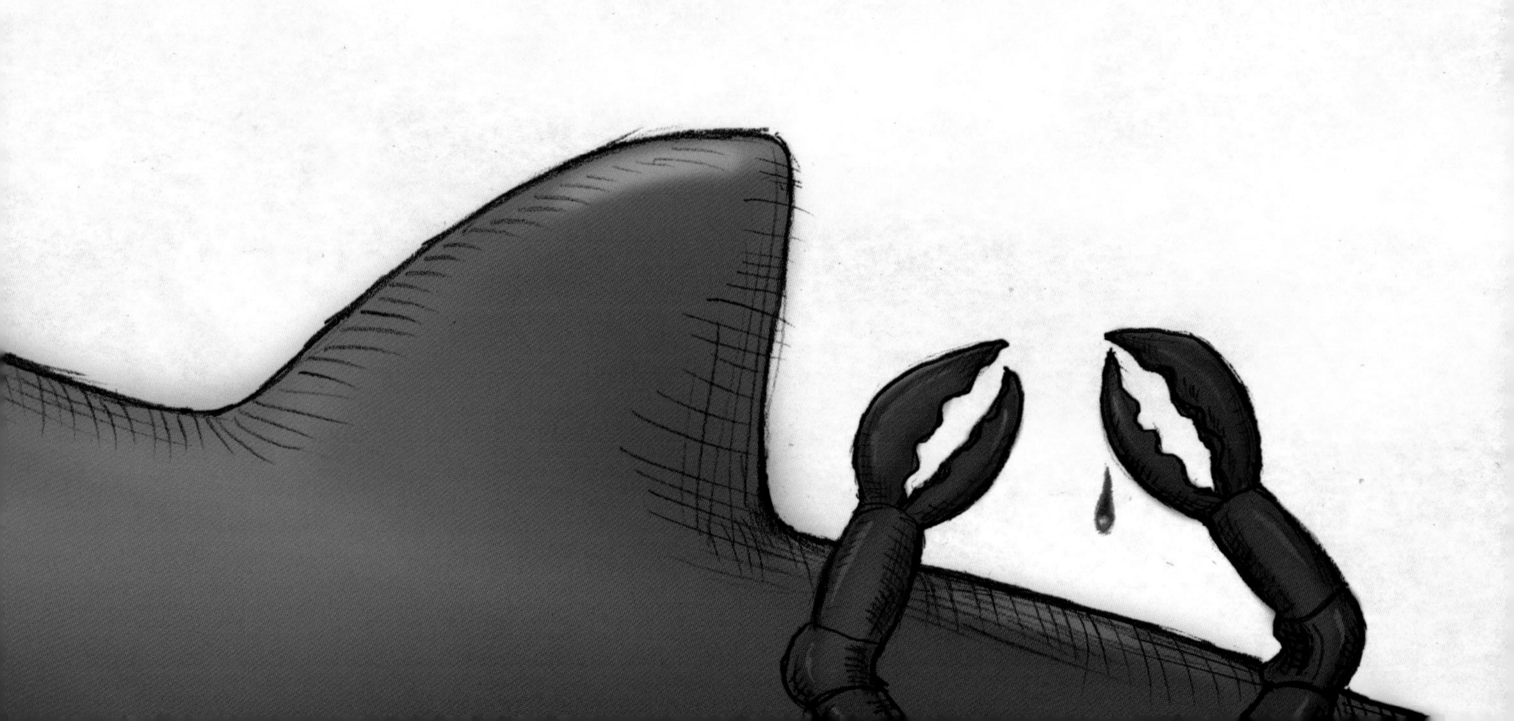

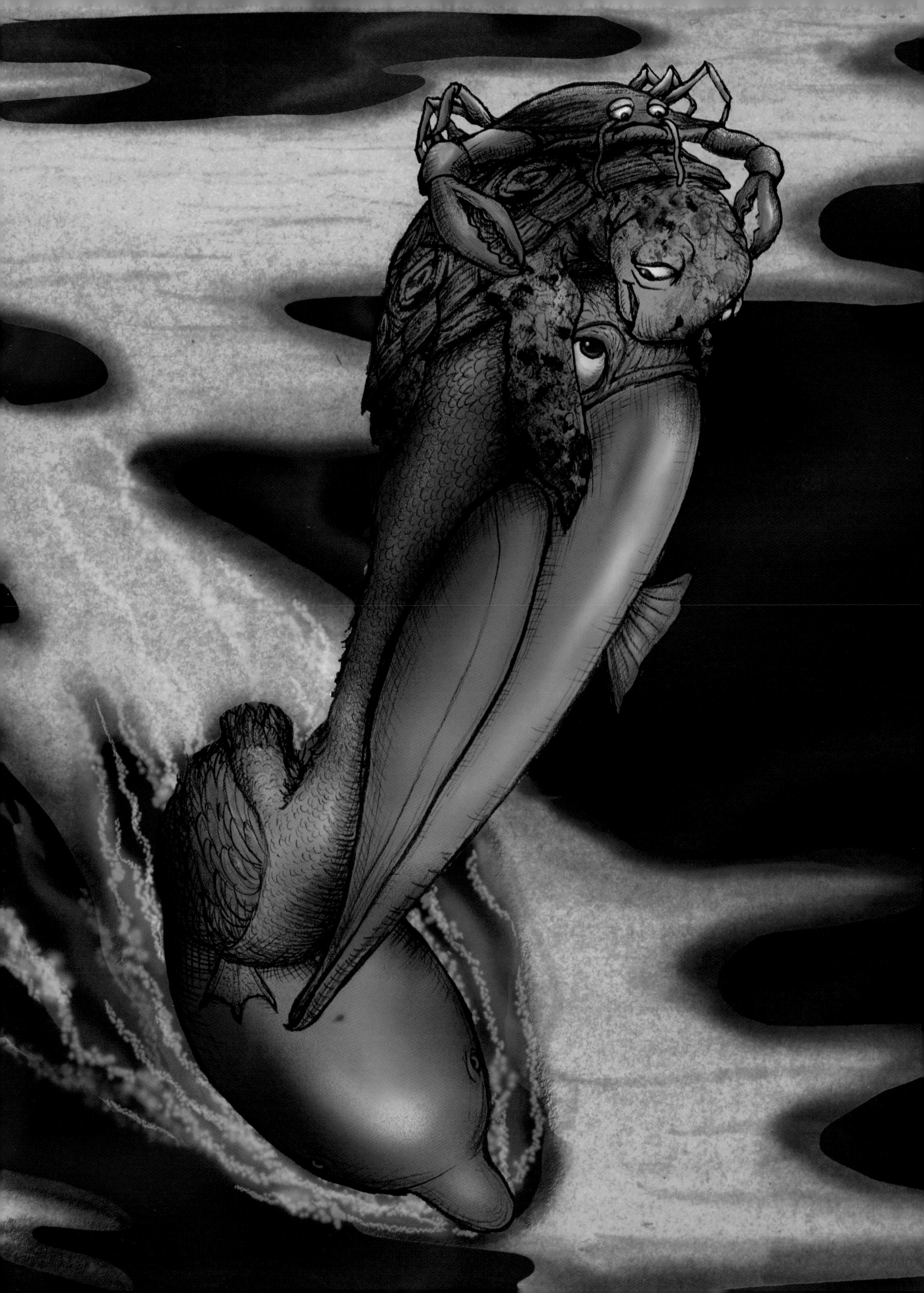

There's a crab on a turtle on a bird
on a dolphin in the oil
on the surface of the sea

A crab on a turtle on a bird
on a dolphin in the oil
on the surface of the sea

All from a hole
All from a hole

From a hole in the bottom of the sea.

There's a windmill up on the hill
A windmill up on the hill

There's a windmill

A windmill

A windmill up on the hill.

There's a generator run by the windmill up on the hill
A generator run by the windmill up on the hill
There's a windmill
It's a wind farm!
A windmill up on the hill.

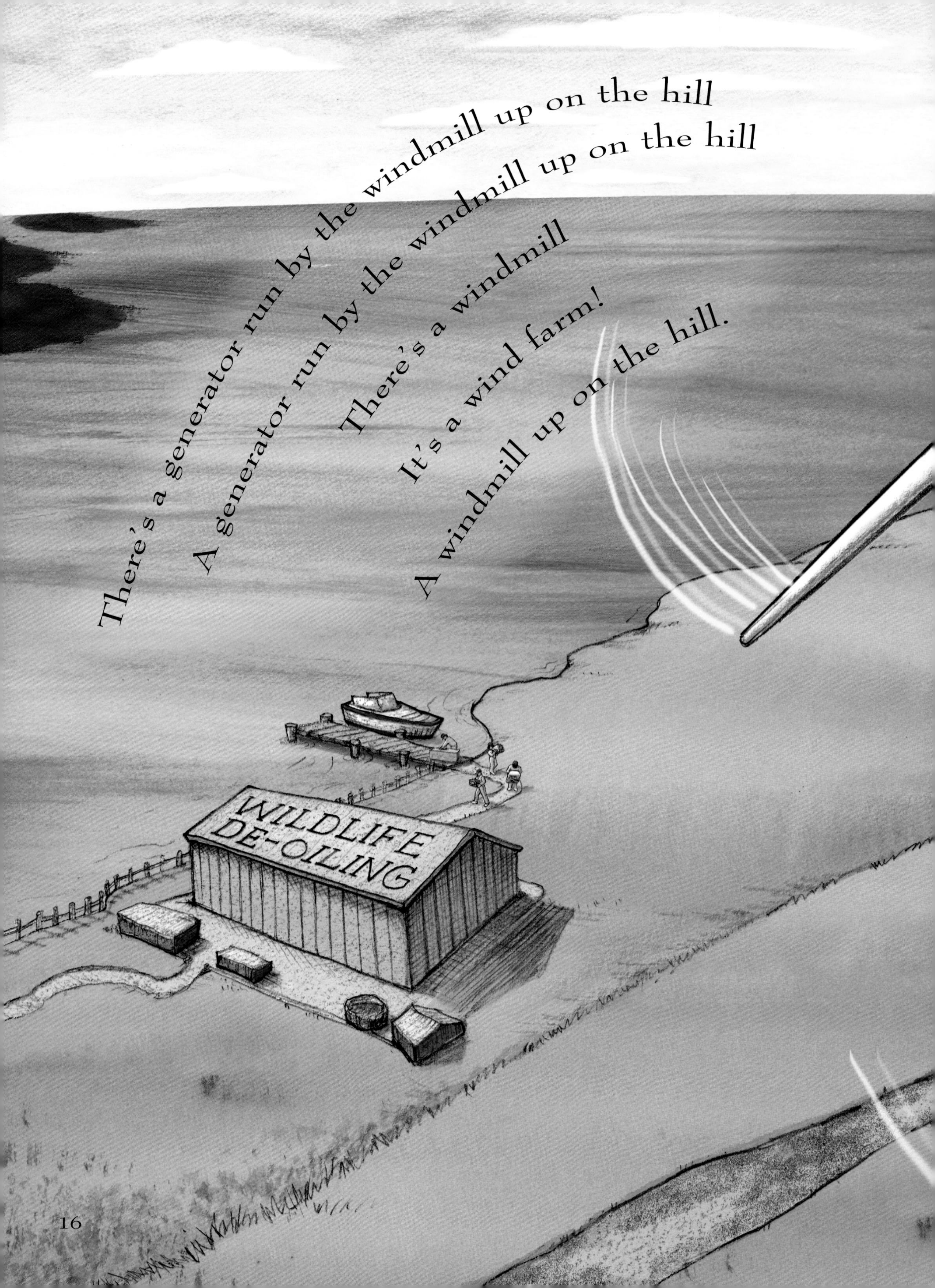

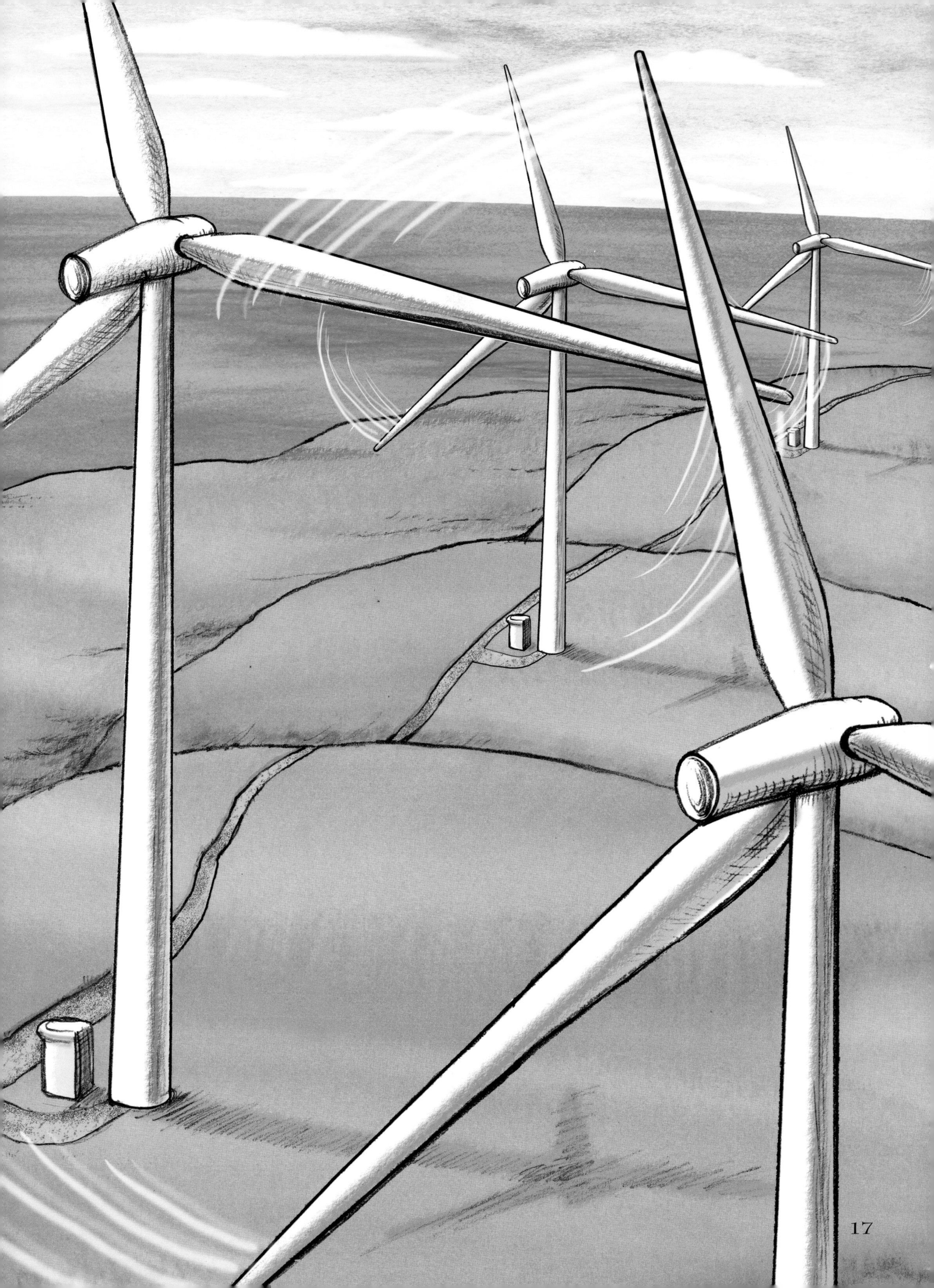

There's water heated by the generator by the windmill up on the hill
Water heated by the generator by the windmill up on the hill
There is water
Heated by the generator
By the windmill up on the hill.

SOAP

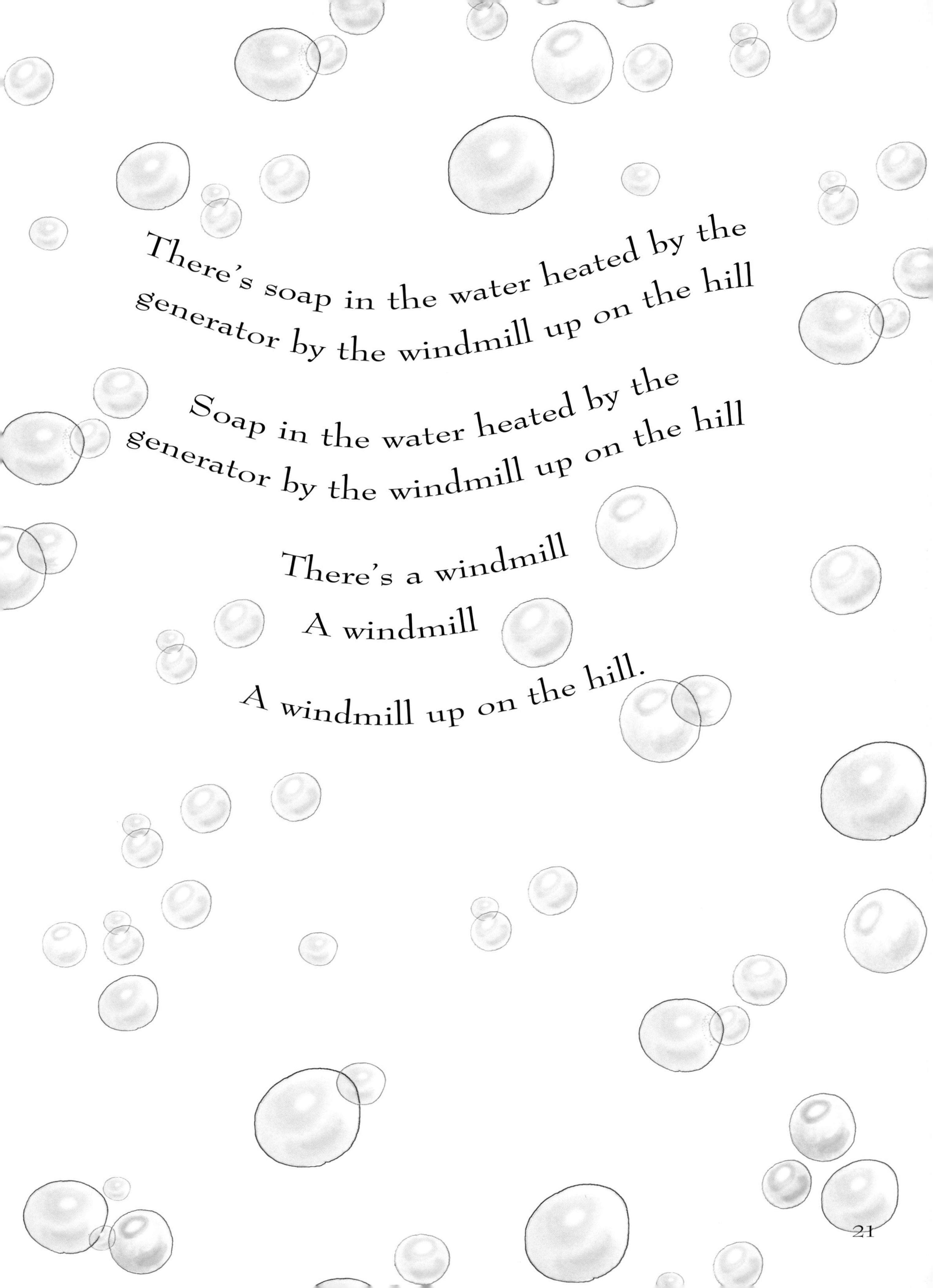

There's soap in the water heated by the
generator by the windmill up on the hill

Soap in the water heated by the
generator by the windmill up on the hill

There's a windmill
A windmill
A windmill up on the hill.

We'll clean the oil off the crab and the turtle
and the bird and the dolphin with the soap
in the water heated by the generator
by the windmill up on the hill

(Sing it again!)

There's a windmill

HOORAY FOR WINDMILLS!

A windmill up on the hill.

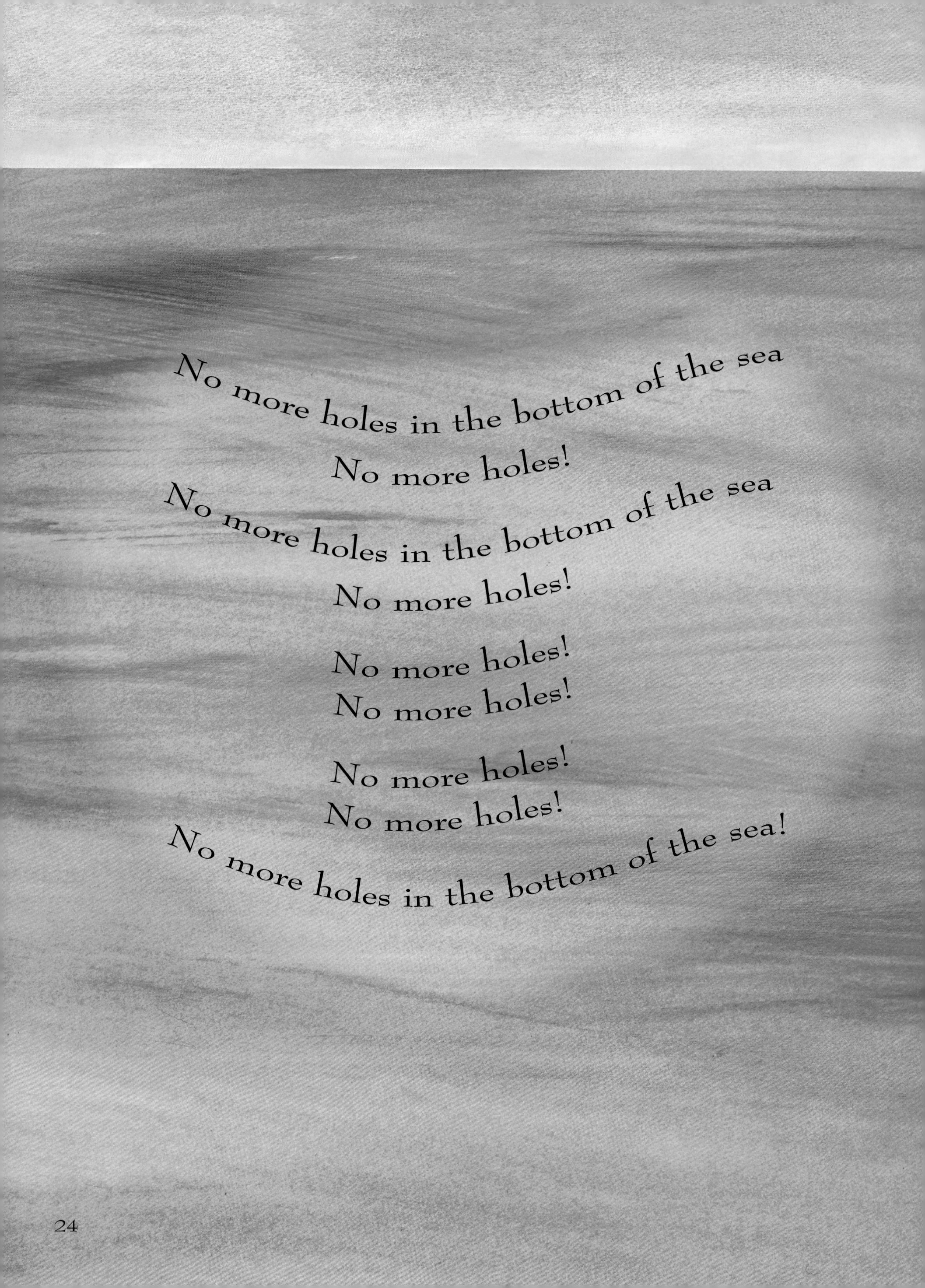

No more holes in the bottom of the sea
No more holes!
No more holes in the bottom of the sea
No more holes!

No more holes!
No more holes!

No more holes!
No more holes!
No more holes in the bottom of the sea!

NO MORE HOLES IN THE BOTTOM OF THE SEA!

How animals are cleaned and rehabilitated

Written by Betsy Franco Feeney

In our song, the animals are caught with a net and brought to a "de-oiling" center. They are washed with warm, soapy water; rinsed; blown dry and then set free in clean water far from the oil spill.

In reality, there are separate centers for different animals to be cleaned and made healthy. For example, when a pelican is brought into a bird rescue center, first a veterinarian examines it to determine the treatment the bird needs. The next step is letting the pelican rest and drink some much-needed clean water. Vets even use blenders to make fish smoothies that pelicans can easily drink – yum! When the birds are stronger, canola oil is spread on them to loosen the thick layer of oil before they are washed with the warm, soapy water. On page 22, we see the crab using a toothbrush to clean himself. In reality, rescuers use toothbrushes to clean the nooks and crannies on the pelicans, too. Then the soap is rinsed off with clean water and their feathers are blown dry. Pelicans cannot be released into the wild for at least one week so the doctors can make sure that they are fully recovered. They get to hang out with other clean pelicans in a little oasis, like a pelican country club complete with their own little pool!

Blue Crabs (*Callinectes sapidus*), named for the blue tint on their legs, are found on the east coasts of North and South America and in the Gulf of Mexico. They eat algae, small plants, clams and fish. During the 2010 Gulf Oil Spill, scientists found that many young crabs (called larvae) had ingested oil. This was a concern not only for people who love to eat crabs but for other animals like birds, fish and raccoons who also feed on crabs. It will take scientists many years to assess how the oil has spread throughout the food chain.

The Kemp's Ridley Sea Turtle (*Lepidochelys kempii*) is the most endangered of the five species of sea turtles found in the Gulf of Mexico and is the smallest of all, with a top shell (carapace) measuring up to 28 inches long. Adults can weigh 100 pounds and live as long as 50 years. They like to eat crabs, jellyfish, clams and fish. During the 2010 Gulf Oil Spill, many sea turtles and their nesting beaches were covered with oil. After the spill, over 70,000 turtle eggs were removed from nesting beaches, incubated in a lab and then released back into the Gulf.

Brown Pelicans (*Pelecanus occidentalis*) are found along the West, East and Gulf Coasts of North America and along the West Coast of South America. Smallest of the eight types of pelicans found worldwide, they have a wingspan of 6 feet and weigh up to 11 pounds as adults. They mainly eat fish and have an interesting way of hovering over the water before plunge-diving to catch fish in their large yellow pouches. During the 2010 Gulf Oil Spill, hundreds of brown pelicans were cleaned, banded and released. The large, colored leg tags will help scientists find and observe these birds in the future.

Bottlenose Dolphins (*Tursiops truncatus*) are found in warm and temperate waters throughout the world. They live in groups of generally ten to thirty individuals and can live for up to 40 years. Bottlenose dolphins feed on small fish that swim in groups called schools. Dolphins, like all other animals, can be harmed by an oil spill through both external exposure (getting the toxic chemicals on their skin) and through ingestion (both from oiled food and accidental swallowing of oiled water).

Why do we have holes in the bottom of the sea?

We need a lot of **energy** to live in a modern world. Energy lets us do work, move things, heat and cool things, and go places. For a human being, food is energy. For many of our modern machines, **electricity** is energy. We get most of our electricity today by burning things called fossil fuels. These are made from tiny plants and animals that lived millions of years ago and are buried under the sea and inside the earth.

Sometimes, in our quest for more energy, accidents happen. One of those unfortunate accidents occurred in the Gulf of Mexico in April of 2010. Many millions of gallons of oil leaked from a broken pipe. Eleven oil workers lost their lives, and many people lost their jobs because the oil in the water destroyed the fish they caught. Also, no one wanted to take vacations at hotels with oil on the beaches. As we see in this book, many animals were also hurt and some even lost their lives.

Scientific research suggests that using fossil fuels for energy has caused other problems around the world. Acid rain falls from the sky, which harms plants and animals. Smog, which is unhealthy air to breathe, chokes our big cities. Also, burning fossil fuels releases what are called "greenhouse gases" into the earth's atmosphere. These gases cause what scientists refer to as climate change — in some places, Earth is warming more quickly than it ever has. If Earth gets too warm, many areas of land along the coast will be underwater as the ice melts at the North and South Poles.

On top of all the negative things that happen by using fossil fuels, someday we will run out of them. That means they are **nonrenewable**. A type of energy that will never be used up and can be used over and over again is called a **renewable** source. Many scientists think the time is overdue to start using renewable energy in a bigger way to ensure a safer and cleaner planet for future generations.

Renewable Energy Forms (Source: U.S. Department of Energy)

Solar

Solar energy comes from the sun. Solar panels can make electricity or heat water, and the sun's heat can warm up your house!

Wind

Big windmills called wind turbines have blades that catch the wind and spin to create electricity.

Geothermal

Geothermal energy comes from hot fluids within Earth's crust, and by moving water through heated zones in the upper crust. Both hot water and steam are used for producing geothermal energy in California, for instance.

Hydropower

We can use the movement of water in our oceans and rivers to spin turbines underwater that are similar to windmills. The spinning of the turbines creates electricity.

Biomass

Biomass comes from corn and other plants that we turn into fuel, including ethanol and biodiesel that we can use to run our cars. We can also make fabric and carpet with biomass!

Windmills and Energy Wind is actually a form of solar energy, because winds are caused by the uneven heating of air by the sun.

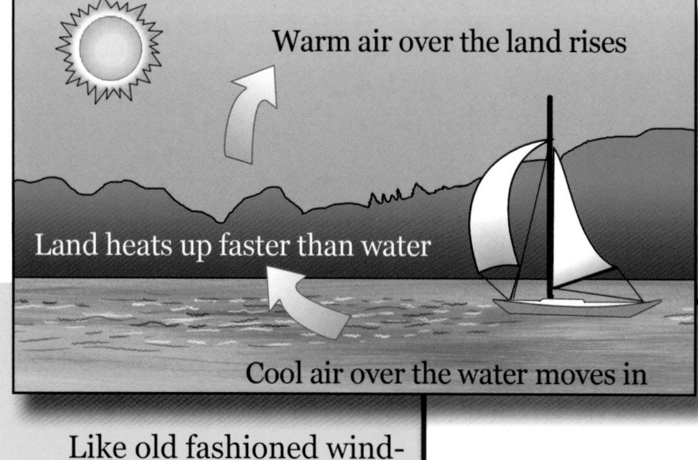

Warm air over the land rises
Land heats up faster than water
Cool air over the water moves in

People used the wind as energy to move boats along the Nile River many thousands of years ago. In the Middle East, they used windmills to grind grain. Early windmills were also used by the Chinese and Dutch to pump water.

Like old fashioned windmills, today's wind turbines use blades to harness the wind's kinetic energy. The wind flows over the blades, creating lift, like the effect of wind on airplane wings.

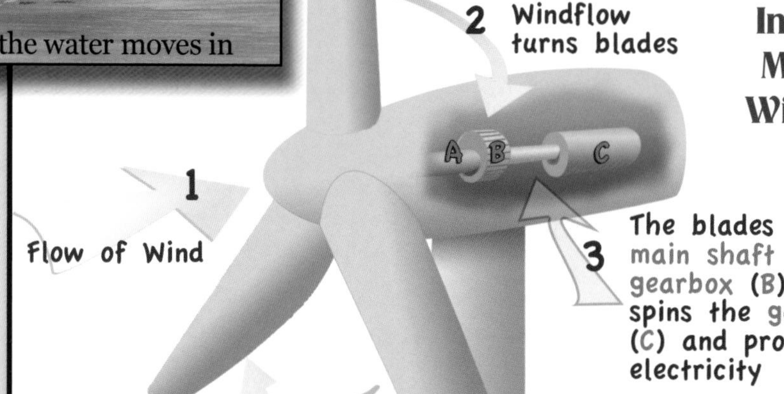

Inside a Modern Windmill
1 Flow of Wind
2 Windflow turns blades
3 The blades spin the main shaft (A) and gearbox (B) which spins the generator (C) and produces electricity
A
B
C

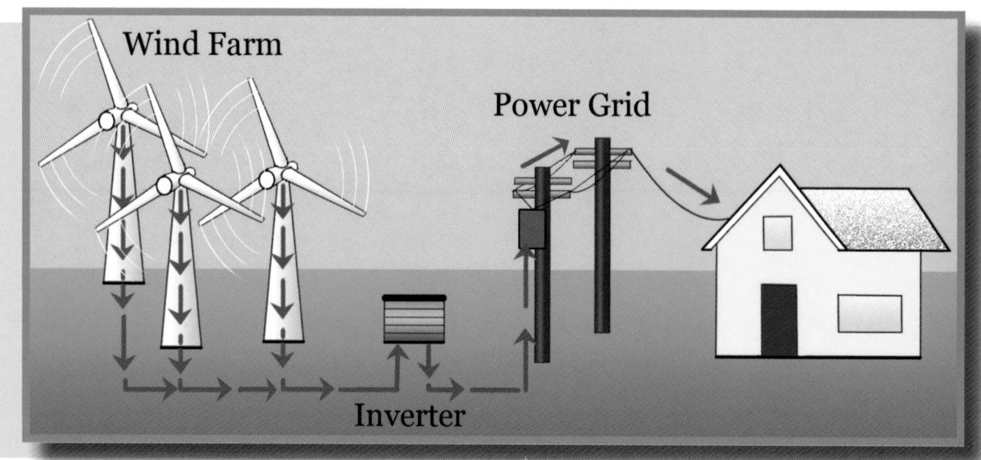

Wind Farm
Power Grid
Inverter

Electricity created by a **wind farm** (a group of wind turbines) is hooked up to a power grid. This grid will send electricity to our homes and businesses through the transmission wires.

Advantages of Using Wind Energy

- As long as the sun shines, there will always be wind.
- Wind energy is safe and clean energy.
- Because of new improvements, wind energy is becoming less expensive to produce in some areas.

Challenges of Using Wind Energy

- With the new wind machines, there is still the problem of what to do when the wind isn't blowing. At those times, other types of power plants must be used to make electricity.
- Some people don't like the look of windmills. Others think they are attractive alternatives to conventional power plants.
- Sometimes birds or bats are harmed when they fly into a wind turbine. As the technology improves, more precautions will be developed to make wind turbines safer for wildlife.

This photo shows the latest technology to harness wind energy at lower wind speeds.

Make a pinwheel and watch it turn in the wind!

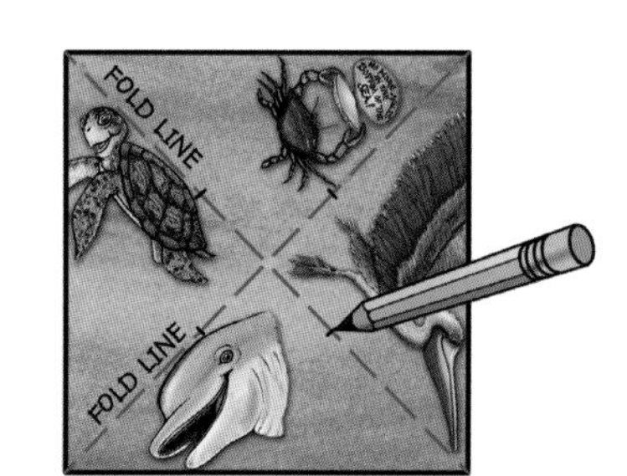

1. Start with a square of paper. You can even re-use a grocery bag or some other paper! You may also print the pattern shown here from the website **www.holeinthebottomofthe sea.com**.

2. Fold your square diagonally, then unfold, for both sides.

3. Make a pencil mark on each fold line about 1/3 of the way from center.

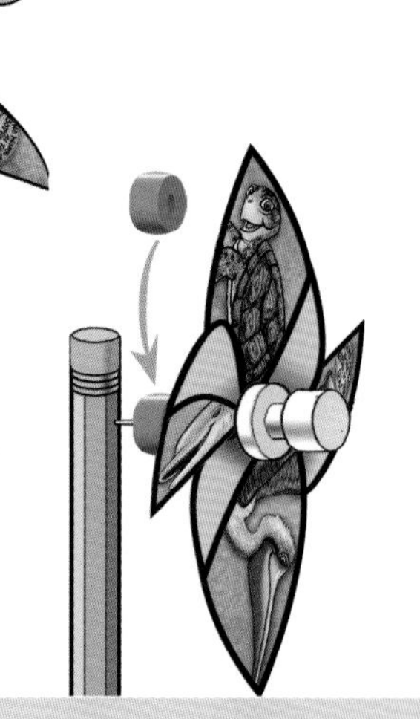

4. Cut along the fold lines, but stop at your pencil mark.

5. Bend into the center every other point, and stick a pushpin through all four points.

6. Flip your pinwheel over – make sure the pin is exactly centered.

7. Spin the pushpin around a few times to make the hole a little bigger so your pinwheel spins easily.

8. Stick the pin into a thin wooden stick – a pencil is perfect!

9. It might help to separate your pinwheel from the pencil with a bead or two for super spinning!

How you can save energy at home

Scientists agree that no matter which form of energy we use, we must use less of it in the future.

Here's a checklist of things you can do around your own home that will save energy:

- Turn off the television and the computer when you are not using them
- Turn off the lights when you leave a room or go out (or better yet, use natural light from the sun!)
- Don't leave the refrigerator door open for a long time
- Recycle cans, glass bottles, plastic containers and paper
- Use an energy-saving fluorescent lightbulb instead of an incandescent one
- Ride your bike to get somewhere instead of having your parents drive you
- Use a hand-operated can opener, not an electric one
- Wear a sweater in the winter to stay warm instead of turning up the thermostat
- Pass down clothes that you have outgrown to a brother or sister or to someone else

Photo Credits for Page 26:
Cleaning the pelican: Courtesy of JT Blatty
Blue crab: Courtesy of Fran Baer
Kemp's ridley sea turtle: Courtesy of National Park Service
Brown pelican: Courtesy of JT Blatty
Bottlenose dolphin: Courtesy of Fran Baer
Photo Credit for Page 28:
Windspire turbine: Courtesy of Windspire Energy, Inc.

Hole in the Bottom of the Sea

Traditional
with new lyrics © 2012 Christine Lavin

*Complete, downloadable sheet music is available at www.holeinthebottomofthesea.com

The Guys & Dolphins All-Starfish Band

The musicians and singers who recorded "Hole in the Bottom of the Sea"
featuring
Christine Lavin, Don White, Claudia Russell, Bruce Kaplan, David Buskin & Robin Batteau, Sandy Cash, Steve Doyle, Ruby Rakos, Colleen McHugh, Ashley Madison and The Ashley Mads 8th Grade Chorus (Oz Bejerano, Victoria Galante, Caroline Haskins, Mia Herrel, Sarah Jordan, Max Kasler, Leah Rousso, Kaitlyn Sanford, Emily Weissman)
with
Sandi Bachom, Judy Brough, Lodi Carr, Joan Crowe, Leslie Danoff, Lois Dino, Bob Dolphin, Margaret Dorn, Steve Doyle, Edith Drake, Ervin Drake, Janet Fanale, Betsy Franco Feeney, Kathryn Feeney, John Forster, Julie Gold, David Goldman, Laura Grunwerg, Nancy Heppner, Phillip Klum, Rob Langeder, Joan Maute, Budd Mishkin, Garry Novikoff, Christine Pedi, John Platt, Sheila Sheffield Platt, Sarah Rice, Ethan Robbins, Larry Robbins, Jenny Lynn Stewart and the band Still Saffire (Charlotte Harrow, Sonya Harrow, Annika Scilipote and Soreya Scilipote)
Produced by Brian Bauers

HITBOTS Kickstarters

The following individuals and groups pledged $100 or more to HITBOTS's funding campaign during the summer of 2011. The creators of this book are forever grateful to them for making this book and song a reality. A list of all kickstarters is available online at www.holeinthebottomofthesea.com.

Tim Abraham & Dawn Walton, Dawn Berg, Rich Borden, Elizabeth Brasser, Judith Brough, Jenny Caldwell, Gerald & Tracy Carcione, Centre for ISO9000, Nikki Chayet, Pearl Chin, Seth Cutler, Leslie Danoff & Larry Robbins, Lois Dino & Ben Epstein, Sally Fingerett & Michael Stan, Jan Fisher & Ian Friedland, Friend of HITBOTS, Karen, Dave, Ben & Sammy Fulmer, Michelle Fury Feuer, Julie Gold, David Hare, Barbara Hooper, Sue Lacroix, Mary Slothower Lavin & Tom Lavin Slothower, Francesca H. Lopez, Darrin Magee & Beth Kinne, Joan & Mark Maute, Erica Miller, Hans Miller, Peter & Mary Beth Modafferi, Nancy Moran, Alan Perry, Judy & Adam Pick, Poltronieri Tang & Associates, Public Domain Foundation, Cindy Reisenauer, Dave & Diane Rumbel, Bev Russell, Rebecca Russell McFee, Julie Anne Sheinman, Tonia Sledd, Jimmy & Melissa Sullivan, Wendy Svenson, Tammy Tsai, United Hospice of Rockland, Inc., Diane Weber, Cheryl Wheeler, Kathleen Whitaker, Linda Yoder

And thanks to the following...
Consultants for the Science Appendix

Dr. Erica Miller
Wildlife Veterinarian & Past President of the National Wildlife Rehabilitators Assoc.

Dr. Darrin Magee
Environmental Studies Professor at Hobart and William Smith Colleges

Dr. Koty Sharp
Marine Biologist at the Ocean Genome Legacy

Dr. Joan Maute
Educator and Singer/Songwriter of earth-friendly songs

Christy Walker
Education Specialist, Farallones Marine Sanctuary Association

Beth Kinne
Attorney and Professor of Environmental Studies at Hobart and William Smith Colleges

Jessica Reichard
GE Renewables

Dr. Al Duba
Geophysicist, Earth and Planetary Sciences at the American Museum of Natural History

Website for this book: www.holeinthebottomofthesea.com

At this website, you will find:

- Links to animal-rescue and clean-energy informational websites
- Links to websites and videos on wind-energy science experiments
- Complete song lyrics and music for both piano and guitar for "Hole in the Bottom of the Sea"
- A printable pattern and instructions for making the pinwheel

Resources for more information

National Oceanic and Atmospheric Administration website on the Deepwater Horizon impact and response
www.noaa.gov/deepwaterhorizon/

U.S. Energy Information Administration site for kids and educators
www.eia.gov/kids

National Wildlife Rehabilitators Association
www.nwrawildlife.org

Department of Energy; Energy Efficiency and Renewable Energy Page
www.eere.energy.gov

Tri-State Bird Rescue & Research
www.tristatebird.org

Windspire Wind Turbines
www.windspireenergy.com

Environmental song download page by Joan Maute, HITBOTS contributor and educator
www.joanmaute.com/page6/page6.html

There are some great experiments for kids relating to oil spills at the Environmental Protection Agency website:
www.epa.gov/students

Specific exercises for middle-school kids can be found at:
www.epa.gov/emergencies/content/learning/midlab.htm

Oiled Wildlife Care Network
www.owcn.org

Note

Hole in the Bottom of the Sea *is a work of fiction and is not meant to literally depict what happened to animals after the 2010 oil spill in the Gulf of Mexico. Artistic license has been taken for the sake of entertainment where the use of wind technology is shown to help clean the animals. The creators of this book have done so with the hope of inspiring children to think about how they can better care for our planet and use our natural resources wisely.*

Visit our other websites:

www.puddlejumppress.com
www.christinelavin.com
www.betsyfrancofeeney.com